Little Cat (

MW00906725

by Carol Pugliano-Martin • illustrated by John Bennett

Little Cat wants to go fast.

Little Cat rides with her mom.
"Is this fast?" says Mom.
"Too slow!" says Little Cat.

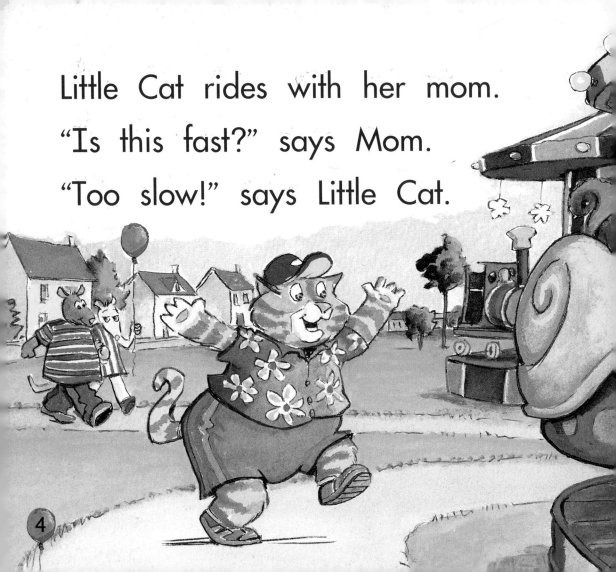

5

Little Cat rides with her dad.
"Is t<u>h</u>is fast?" says Dad.
"Too slow!" says Little Cat.

6

"Is this ride fast?"
Mom and Dad say.
"Too slow!" says Little Cat.

9

Little Cat wants to go
on this ride.

11

Up, up, up they go.

13

Down, down, down they go!

15

Little Cat likes this ride!
Mom and Dad say,
"Too fast!"